For everyone at Pan de *Marseille* workshop, especially Flo, for her expertise in earthworms and other crazy creatures!

MARIE-ÉLISE MASSON

Marie-Élise Masson

NOT SO FAST,
Gigi Giraffe!

AUZOU

It was a cold, grey Monday, and Gigi Giraffe was choosing what to wear for her daily cycle ride.

She wanted to feel special, so she picked out her brand-new red jumper.

As she set off, she spotted Mila Mouse struggling to carry a large stack of boxes.

Was Mila wearing *the same brand-new red jumper*? Suddenly, Gigi didn't feel special at all.

"COPYCAT!" she yelled as she zoomed past.

On Tuesday, Gigi picked out the tartan skirt she had bought on holiday in Scotland. It made her feel like she was still on holiday!

Was that Heidi Hippo wearing *the same tartan skirt*? Suddenly, Gigi didn't feel like she was on holiday any more…

"COPYCAT!" she hissed at Heidi as she whooshed past.

On Wednesday, Gigi slipped on the long, shiny boots her Canadian cousin had sent her as a birthday present. They made her feel like it was still her birthday! She set off.

Was that Tara Tortoise wearing *the same long, shiny boots*? Suddenly, Gigi didn't feel like it was her birthday any more.

"COPYCAT!" she snarled at Tara as she sped past.

On Thursday, Gigi felt gloomy. To cheer herself up, she put on her softest silk scarf. It made her feel elegant. As she cycled down the street, she saw Christina Crocodile. Was Christina wearing *the same soft silk scarf*? Suddenly, Gigi didn't feel elegant at all.

"**COPYCAT!**" she shrieked at Christina as she flew past.

On Friday, Gigi felt shy. She put on her favourite dress. It was bright red with white spots, and always made her feel confident. As she cycled down the street, she caught a glimpse of something red and white...
Was Lily Lemur wearing *the same bright red dress with white spots*?
Suddenly, Gigi didn't feel confident at all.

"COPYCAT!" she muttered angrily at Lily as she rushed past.

"HELP!"

On Saturday, Gigi woke up determined to prove to everyone that she was special, elegant and confident.
She put on her very best hat. She bought it in London, and it made her feel like a queen!
Gigi had just set off on her bike when she saw Ellie Earthworm...

OWW!

The animals gathered to decide what to do.

"All week, we have needed help, and Gigi hasn't helped any of us. Why should we help her?"

"What shall we do? Should we help her?"

"No way! She never helps anybody else!"

"She's only interested in how she looks!"

"Hello, Gigi, what a lovely hat that is." said Ellie Earthworm timidly.

"What? Can't you see that I need help?" Gigi said crossly.

"And you had such a nice dress on yesterday…" said Lily Lemur.

"What on earth are you talking about?" Gigi snapped.

"And lovely boots on Wednesday!" added Tara Tortoise.

"Why are you thinking about my clothes? I need help!" cried Gigi.

Heidi Hippo sighed. "But Gigi, we all needed help this week, and you were too busy thinking about your clothes to help any of us! Friendship is about helping each other."

Gigi looked sad as she thought about this. "I'm sorry, everyone. I've been a terrible friend. I don't deserve your help."

"Oh, Gigi!" Heidi smiled. "Didn't you listen? Friendship is about helping each other! Let's get you up."

"OK, everyone, on the count of three…"

1…

2…

…3!

"YOU'RE RIGHT," Gigi said.

"Clothes don't matter at all – it's my friends that help me feel my best! Tomorrow, I'm going to have a party to thank you all for being so kind. Who wants to come?"

And everybody did.

© 2021, AUZOU
All rights reserved for all countries.
First published as *Laissez passer Madame Giraffe !*

auzou.co.uk